The Snail
and the
Whale

About the author and illustrator:

Julia Donaldson has written some of the world's favourite picture books. She also writes books for older children, as well as plays and songs, and she spends a lot of time on stage performing her brilliant sing-along shows! Just like the snail and the whale, Julia likes to travel and used to busk around France and Italy with her husband, Malcolm.

Axel Scheffler is a star of children's illustration and has many books to his name which are popular all over the world. Axel grew up in Hamburg in Germany where he loved to go to the port and dream of visiting far away lands. But unlike the snail, Axel only got as far as England!

For everyone at Hillhead Primary School, Wick ~ J.D.

First published 2003 by Macmillan Children's Books
This edition published 2013 by Macmillan Children's Books
a division of Macmillan Publishers Limited
20 New Wharf Road, London N1 9RR
Basingstoke and Oxford
Associated companies throughout the world
www.panmacmillan.com

ISBN: 978-1-4472-3487-6

Text copyright © Julia Donaldson 2003
Illustrations copyright © Axel Scheffler 2003
Moral rights asserted

2 4 6 8 9 7 5 3 1

A CIP catalogue record for this book is available from the British Library.

Printed in China

The Snail and the Whale

Julia Donaldson

Illustrated by Axel Scheffler

MACMILLAN CHILDREN'S BOOKS

This is a tale of a tiny snail
And a great big, grey-blue humpback whale.

This is a rock as black as soot,
And this is a snail with an itchy foot.

The sea snail slithered all over the rock
And gazed at the sea and the ships in the dock.
And as she gazed she sniffed and sighed.
"The sea is deep and the world is wide!
How I long to sail!"
Said the tiny snail.

These are the other snails in the flock,
Who all stuck tight to the smooth black rock
And said to the snail with the itchy foot,
"Be quiet! Don't wriggle! Sit still! Stay put!"
But the tiny sea snail sighed and sniffed,
Then cried, "I've got it! I'll hitch a lift!"

This is the trail
Of the tiny snail,
A silvery trail that looped and curled

And said . . .

Lift wanted around the world

This is the whale who came one night
When the tide was high and the stars were bright.
A humpback whale, immensely long,
Who sang to the snail a wonderful song
Of shimmering ice and coral caves
And shooting stars and enormous waves.

And this is the tail
Of the humpback whale.
He held it out of the starlit sea
And said to the snail,
   "Come sail with me."

This is the sea,
So wild and free,
That carried the whale
And the snail on his tail
To towering icebergs and far-off lands,

With fiery mountains and golden sands.

These are the waves that arched and crashed,
That foamed and frolicked and sprayed
  and splashed
The tiny snail
On the tail of the whale.

These are the caves
Beneath the waves,
Where stripy fish with feathery fins
And sharks with hideous toothy grins
Swam round the whale
And the snail on his tail.

This is the sky
So vast and high,
Sometimes sunny and blue and warm,
Sometimes filled with a thunderstorm,

With zigzag lightning
Flashing and frightening
The tiny snail
On the tail of the whale.

And she gazed at the sky, the sea, the land,
The waves and the caves and the golden sand,

She gazed and gazed, amazed by it all,
And she said to the whale, "I feel so small."

But then came the day
The whale lost his way . . .

These are the speedboats, running a race,
Zigging and zooming all over the place,
Upsetting the whale with their earsplitting roar,
Making him swim too close to the shore.

This is the tide, slipping away . . .

And this is the whale lying beached in a bay.

"Quick! Off the sand! Back to sea!"
     cried the snail.
"I can't move on land! I'm too **big!**"
     moaned the whale.

The snail felt helpless and terribly small.
Then, "I've got it!" she cried, and started to crawl.

"I must not fail,"
Said the tiny snail.

This is the bell on the school in the bay,
Ringing the children in from their play.

This is the teacher, holding her chalk,
Telling the class, "Sit straight! Don't talk!"
This is the board, as black as soot . . .

And this is the snail with the itchy foot!
"A snail! A snail!"
The teacher turns pale.
"Look!" say the children. "It's leaving a trail."
This is the trail
Of the tiny snail,
A silvery trail saying . . .

These are the children, running from school,

Fetching the firemen, digging a pool,

Squirting and spraying to keep the whale cool.

This is the tide coming into the bay,

And these are the villagers shouting, "Hooray!"
As the whale and the snail travel safely away . . .

Back to the dock
And the flock on the rock,
Who said, "How time's flown!"
And, "Haven't you grown!"

And the whale and the snail
Told their wonderful tale
Of shimmering ice and coral caves,
And shooting stars and enormous waves,
And of how the snail, so small and frail,
With her looping, curling, silvery trail,
Saved the life of the humpback whale.

Then the humpback whale
Held out his tail
And on crawled snail after snail after snail.

And they sang to the sea as they all set sail

On the tail of the grey-blue humpback whale.